THE NAPPING QUILT

WRITTEN BY **GARY DEI ROSSI**

ILLUSTRATED BY **MICHAEL HIRSHON**

The Napping Quilt: A Family's Story of Coming to America
Story © Gary Dei Rossi
Illustrations © Michael Hirshon

ISBN-13: 978-0692661413 Lucky Jenny Publishing. Plymouth, California

This book was written to share one family's journey to America and the personal characteristics necessary to reach their goals.

Dedication

This book is dedicated to all the immigrants that came to America to create a better life for themselves and their families. Their contributions to this nation have forged its greatness.

Acknowledgments

Completing a project like this requires the support, cooperation, and encouragement of many people. Although words cannot adequately express my sincere thanks, I would like to recognize the following people for their assistance.

Erica Dei Rossi and Judi Wilson for reviewing and editing the text.

My illustrator Mike Hirshon for all his insights, discussions, talents and drafts.

Elizabeth Chapin-Pinotti, my fellow Bruin that helped this book become a reality.

To Kathy, Kyle, Megan, Eric, Janice and Lou for their support and encouragement.

Megan arrives at her grandmother's house, whom she
affectionately calls Nana.

"Megan you look tired from
your long journey today. You
could use a short nap. Go get
the napping quilt in the family
room," Megan's Nana asks.

With a quizzical look Megan
says, "I am a little tired but
why do we call it the napping
quilt?"

"People in our family have taken naps under this quilt for almost 70 years. It brings warmth, comfort, and tells about the journey my mother, your great grandmother, and I made coming to this country.

On the quilt there are 12 squares that have designs on them. Each describes a part of our life and our journey to America."

"My mother and I were the first people to take a nap under this quilt when we came across America on a train. The quilt was not finished but it provided warmth and comfort just like today."

6

"What does this first square on the quilt show?"
asks Megan.

"Do you mean the one with the mountains,
river and old wooden bridge?" asks Nana.

"Yes that one," replies Megan.

"This square shows your great grandmother's hometown. She would often say that looking at that square reminded her of swimming in the river on hot days in the cool blue water. The bridge reminded her of racing her brothers from one end to the other. She told me she won all the races even though she was younger than them."

"Your great grandmother was athletic and energetic."

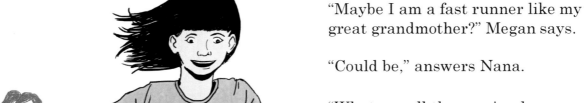

"Maybe I am a fast runner like my great grandmother?" Megan says.

"Could be," answers Nana.

"What are all those animals in the second square?" asks Megan.

"Your great grandmother's parents were farmers and they owned cows, horses, goats, and chickens. In the winter, the animals stayed with them in a barn by their home. In the summer, when the weather was hot in their valley, they took all the animals to the cooler mountains, where they had a small ranch. Your great grandmother often mentioned that it took over a day to hike with all these animals to the ranch. Her favorite thing to do on the trip was eating a warm lunch at her favorite restaurant half-way up the mountain."

"Your great grandmother was healthy and hard-working."

"What are all the buildings in this next square? asks Megan

"This part of the quilt shows your great grandmother's town square. The buildings are her church, the courthouse, and the many stores where she and her family shopped."

"What, no mall?" Megan asked.

Nana replies, "Back then, everyone went to the town
square everyday for their vegetables, fruit, meat,
bread, and fresh water. Your great grandmother said
she loved walking through the square smelling the
freshly baked bread and drinking the sweet clear
water from the fountain."

"Your great grandmother was practical and
appreciative."

"Why are all the buildings so dark and gray?" Megan asks.

"The buildings are made of stone and were built a long time ago. When it is windy and rainy the water washes away a little bit of the stone. Over the years some pollution from fireplaces and cars has mixed with the rain and floats up with the wind and sticks to the buildings—making them look gray and dirty."

"The next square looks like two people are on a bicycle like mine," says Megan.

"Yes, that is your great grandmother and her future husband. They would often ride their bicycles for miles to get to the town square. Few people had cars then because they were so expensive. Once they arrived in the town square they would shop, enjoy a nice meal and if they had enough money buy an ice cream. Her favorite flavor was chocolate with small pieces of candy in it."

"Your great grandmother was affectionate and thrifty."

"The next square shows a big boat. Did they take a cruise?" Megan asks.

"No, that is the ship your great grandmother took across the Atlantic Ocean on her way to New York City. She needed to leave her homeland because there were no jobs, not much food to eat, and no opportunity for a bright future."

"Your great grandmother was adventurous and positive."

"How long did the trip take?" Megan asks.

"It took six weeks and it was a very difficult journey.
The seas were often very rough and many people got sick.
The cabins where people slept were very small and dark. The food was not always warm and did not always taste good. The trip was not like the cruise you went on last year with your family. There were no shore excursions, no buffets, no entertainment and the days were long and cold."

"Your great grandmother was tenacious and persistent."

"So Nana, why would she want to take such an awful trip? Didn't she like her home?" asks Megan.

"She loved her hometown and her friends but she did not see a future for herself, where she was living. She wanted to come to a country that had opportunity for herself and her future children, a land where if you worked hard you could enjoy a good life, and a land that appreciated everyone for their individual worth. She made many sacrifices for her children and future generations like us."

"Your great grandmother was brave and courageous."

"Isn't that the Statue of Liberty?" asks Megan.

"Yes, your great grandmother was so moved by the big beautiful statue she stitched this square. The statue represented the hope of a better life in America and welcomed her to her new home. She told me she cried for many minutes holding me as we passed by the statue. At that moment my mother, your great grandmother realized she had made the right choice and was filled with hope."

"Your great grandmother was patriotic and optimistic."

24

"I know what the next square is." Megan says.
"It is Uncle Dante's train set he puts up at Christmas."

"Actually it is the train your great grandmother rode
across America from New York City to San Francisco."

"Why didn't they fly on a plane?" Megan asks.

"It was not possible to fly. Only trains were available. The trip took
three days and because we did not have a lot of money, we had to
sleep in our seats. There was nothing to do on the train except look
out the window at the beautiful scenery."

"Your great grandmother was fearless and determined."

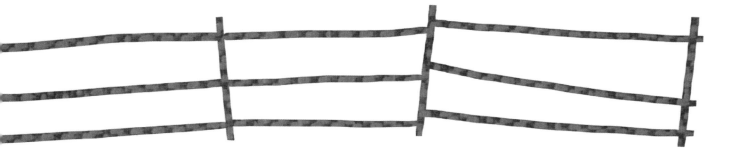

"The next square looks like brown waves. What is it?" Megan asks.

"Those brown waves are fields of wheat. Your great grandmother was amazed about the amount of wheat being grown in the great plains of America. She loved the color and the idea that people could grow so much food. There were times in her hometown that food was not available and people went hungry."

"Your great grandmother was grateful and hopeful."

"This square has a lake. What is it?" asks Megan.

"This part of the quilt shows the great Sierra Nevada Mountains of California and Lake Tahoe. Your great grandmother loved these mountains because it reminded her of home and she thought Lake Tahoe was one of the most beautiful places on Earth."

"I have been to Lake Tahoe many times and I have hiked, canoed, and played miniature golf. I love swimming in the cool clear water in Meeks Bay," says Megan.

"Your great grandmother was intelligent and loved the outdoors."

"What is the city in the next square?" inquires Megan.

"This square represents San Francisco, your great grandmother's new hometown. She loved the weather in San Francisco, the beautiful parks, the museums, the cable cars and the wonderful restaurants."

"Your great grandmother was wise and content."

"Who is in this last square?" asks Megan.

"This square shows all her grandchildren and future generations that would live in America," replies Nana.

But I never met her, how did she know what I would be like?" says Megan.

"That is right. She never knew you but she dreamed of you and believed in a wonderful future for you," says Nana.

"Now it is time for your nap."

"Your great grandmother was a planner and a dreamer."

About the Author

Dr. Gary F. Dei Rossi is the retired Deputy Superintendent of the San Joaquin County Office of Education in Stockton, California. Dr. Dei Rossi has been a classroom teacher, vice principal, principal, district office administrator, and a university adjunct professor. He earned his BA in History from UCLA, an MA in School Management from the University of La Verne and a Doctorate from the University of the Pacific in Educational Administration.

During his career, he was very involved in early childhood education and history-social science curriculum development. He loves to travel, read historical fiction, work in his yard, and watch soccer.

This is his second children's book. His first book, "The ABC Book of San Joaquin County" was written in 2012 with Sue de Polo. It highlights the history, geography, cultural, and economic facts concerning California's San Joaquin County.

Gary is married to Kathy, a retired elementary teacher. Their two adult children both work in education. Gary enjoys sharing his love of literature with his grandchildren.

About the Illustrator

After a nomadic childhood spent doodling, eating, sleeping, and growing, Michael Hirshon ended up as an illustrator. He holds an MFA in Illustration as Visual Essay from the School of Visual Arts.

He has worked with numerous clients including The New York Times, Amazon, American Express, and The Washington Post. Michael's work has been recognized by the Society of Illustrators, 3×3, American Illustration, Creative Quarterly, CMYK, Gestalten, and the AIGA.

Made in the USA
Las Vegas, NV
22 March 2024

87615137R00026